ON GUARD

BY JAKE MADDOX

ILLUSTRATED BY SEAN TIFFANY

text by Eric Stevens

STONE ARCH BOOKS
a capstone imprint

Jake Maddox Books are published by Stone Arch Books
A Capstone Imprint
1710 Roe Crest Drive
North Mankato, Minnesota 56003
www.capstonepub.com

Library of Congress Cataloging-in-Publication data is available on the Library
of Congress website.

Library Binding: 978-1-4342-1920-6
Paperback: 978-1-4342-2279-4

CREATIVE DIRECTOR: Heather Kindseth
ART DIRECTOR: Kay Fraser
GRAPHIC DESIGNER: Hilary Wacholz
PRODUCTION SPECIALIST: Michelle Biedscheid

Printed and bound in the United States of America.
010564R

TABLE OF CONTENTS

Team JAKE MADDOX

WILLY WILDCAT, COACH T, TREY, DANIEL, DWAYNE, ISAAC, PJ

#		Position	PPG	FT %	FG %	Stl	Re...
	Danny Powell	Center	9	73.2	82.8	5	22
11	Daniel Friedland	Forward	5.7	95.8	85.1	12	10
13	PJ Harris	Center	22	65.6	90.2	7	32
23	Trey Smith ⓒ	Guard	14	96.2	80.5	20	8
26	Isaac Roth	Guard	11.5	94.1	79.3	11	6
33	Dwayne Illy	Forward	6.2	82.9	77.9	9	13

Athlete Highlight: **Trey Smith**

Trey Smith is the Wildcats team captain. His free throw accuracy is amazing, but his rebound ability is lacking. He has lots of passion on the court. To beat Trey, a team needs to get to him emotionally.

Chapter 1
SMITH
SMITHEREENS

On the last weekend of the summer, a banner hung across the gate at the entrance to Harding County Park, just outside of Westfield. The big sign read, "Smith Family Reunion."

Just past the gate, dozens of cars were parked in the lot. There were sedans, new and old; station wagons covered in bumper stickers; SUVs, some shiny, some covered in mud.

And just past the lot, near the picnic tables, cousins Trey and Pete Smith were leaning back on their bench. Each boy was holding a paper cup. They were taking a break from their basketball game.

"Ready?" eighth-grader Trey asked. He crushed his paper cup in his hand, then threw it into a nearby garbage can. "Two points."

Pete, who was in sixth grade, took a long drink from his own cup. "Ahh," he said. "Grandma's lemonade is so good." Then he jumped up, crushed his cup, and shot it toward the garbage can. It went in.

"I'm ready," Pete said.

Together, the two boys walked out of the shade and headed over to the basketball courts.

Most of the other Smith family boys, and several of the girls, were hanging around. Some were just watching, but others were taking some shots.

"Look out, everybody. We're back," Trey announced.

"So, any more challengers?" Pete added. "The Smith Smithereens are ready to play some more two-on-two."

Pete, though he wasn't the oldest cousin, was one of the best basketball players in the family. And when he teamed up with Trey — like he always did — no one could beat them.

"We'll take you two on," a voice said. Trey and Pete turned around. It was Uncle Rob and his daughter Jessa. "Jessa and I have been practicing," Uncle Rob added.

Trey and Pete laughed and high-fived each other. "No problem," Trey said. He called over to one of his cousins for the ball. "Let's do it."

Uncle Rob and Jessa started with the ball. Rob was much taller than both boys, and Jessa, who was fifteen, was as tall as Trey.

Still, when Rob took his first shot, Pete jumped up and knocked the ball right into Trey's hands.

"Ha!" Pete shouted. "That was a nice shot, Uncle Rob."

Trey drove the ball fast up the court and scored an easy two points.

Rob and Jessa looked at each other and rolled their eyes, but that didn't stop Trey and Pete.

The cousins continued to shoot and score. After every basket, block, or steal, the two Smith boys would high-five and holler. They felt great, and they quickly had an unbeatable lead.

By the time the game was over, the score was 21 to 4. Trey's dad had shown up to watch the end. He stood on the sidelines next to Uncle Theo, Pete's dad.

"Well, there's no doubt about it," Uncle Rob said. He looked worn out. "You two are a great team."

"Thanks," Pete said, smiling.

"I wonder, though," Trey's father said. "What would happen if these two played against each other for once?"

"Might be interesting to see," Uncle Theo agreed.

"Pff," Trey said, waving them off. He threw an arm around his cousin's shoulder. "We'll never play against each other. Me and Pete, we're a team."

Pete nodded. "Right," he said. "Together, we'll beat anyone."

Chapter 2
SIXTH-GRADE STARTER

At the end of the first week of school, the Westfield Middle School basketball team held tryouts.

No one was surprised when Trey was named starting shooting guard and captain of the team.

The night of the tryouts, Trey went home and went straight to his family computer. He had to tell his cousin Pete the good news.

Hey, Pete, Trey typed in his instant message program.

What's up, cuz? Pete replied.

Guess who's going to be captain of the Westfield Middle School basketball team this season? Trey typed. *And starting shooting guard.*

Pete typed back, *Way to go, Trey. But guess what? I'm starting shooting guard for Eastlake, and I'm only in sixth grade. Ha!*

Trey couldn't believe it. He knew his cousin Pete was a great basketball player, but starting in sixth grade? That was pretty much unheard of.

Trey hadn't been a starter until he was in seventh grade, and most players he knew didn't start until eighth grade, if they got to start at all.

Wow! Trey typed. *That's amazing, Pete.*

You know what this means, right? Pete typed. *Our dads are going to get their wish.*

What wish? Trey typed.

To see us play against each other for once, Pete replied.

Trey grabbed his backpack from the couch and pulled out the papers Coach Turnbull had given him. He quickly flipped through them until he found the one titled "Schedule."

He ran his finger down the page, but didn't have to look far.

Oh man! he typed to his cousin. *The Wildcats play Eastlake. Next week!*

Chapter 3
IT'S ON!

Early that Saturday morning, Trey and Pete met at a local park. They often did, to challenge other guys to two-on-two games. Just like at the family reunion, they rarely lost.

Pete was on the court, shooting free throws, when Trey walked up. "Hey, cuz," Trey said.

Pete spun around and smiled. "Think fast," he said.

He passed the ball to Trey. It moved like a rocket, but Trey was quick. He caught the pass, and the ball made a loud slap as it hit his palms.

Trey smiled back, then glanced at the hoop. He raised the ball, drew it back, and shot.

Swish!

"For three!" Trey said. He jogged over to the basket and grabbed the ball.

Pete held up his hands for a pass. "Give it here," he said. "Still too early for two-on-two, I guess."

"Yeah," Trey said. "No one else is around."

Trey passed the ball to Pete. "We can just shoot around until some other people show up," Trey said.

Pete took a shot from the baseline for two. "Swish!" he called as the ball fell. "I have a better idea."

Trey grabbed the rebound and dribbled up to the foul line. "What?" he asked. Then he made a perfect free throw.

"Let's play some one-on-one," Pete said. He jogged to the basket and picked up the ball before it rolled onto the grass around the court. "It will be like a sneak preview for next week's game."

Trey narrowed his eyes at his cousin. "That could be fun," he said. "You can start, since I have the advantage in, let's see . . ." Trey counted off on his fingers, "Height, age, skill, good looks . . ."

"Ha ha," Pete replied. He dribbled up the foul line. "You ready?"

Trey smiled and nodded. "Bring it, young fella," he said.

Pete faked a shot, but didn't fool Trey at all. Then Pete started to his left and went right.

That didn't fool Trey either. He knew Pete so well, he knew there was no way Pete was going left. Pete was always much faster moving to his right.

Trey stayed with him to the basket, but Pete managed to sink the layup.

"Good D, cuz," Pete said.

Trey grabbed the ball and took it to the line.

"Not good enough, though," Pete added with a smirk.

Trey grunted. "Just watch this," he said.

The two boys played one-on-one all morning. Even when some other guys showed up for two-on-two, Trey and Pete didn't stop their tournament. They played game after game to 21 points, and neither of them ever won by much.

The boys decided to play one more game before lunch. Soon, the score was 20 to 20. It was Trey's possession.

Trey glanced at the basket, faked a shot, and then went to his left. But Pete was quick. He knocked the ball out of Trey's hand.

Before Trey could react, Pete had grabbed the ball and was running toward the hoop. He made the layup easily and won the game.

"Ha!" Pete shouted.

All the guys watching were laughing and hooting and hollering.

"I won!" Pete yelled. "I beat Trey, one-on-one."

Pete grabbed the ball and dribbled it over to Trey. He was really showing off, doing tricks like dribbling between his legs.

"Whatever," Trey said. He took a swig from his water bottle. "We've been playing all morning."

Pete laughed. "So?" he said.

Trey turned to the other guys watching. "We both won some, we both lost some," he said. "So what if he won that game, right? Just one game."

Pete came running over. "That was the last game," Pete said. "So that's the one that matters."

Trey turned to his cousin. "Oh yeah?" he said. "Let's see how it goes next week. Westfield will destroy Eastlake."

"Oooh," said a few of the guys watching.

Pete glared at his cousin. "We'll see," he said.

"Right, we will," Trey replied. Then he turned and walked off. "I'm going home."

Chapter 4
PRACTICE

The rest of the weekend went by quickly. Soon Trey was back at basketball practice with the Wildcats. As shooting guard, it was often Trey's job to get the ball in the hoop. Most plays meant Isaac Roth, the starting point guard, would look for Trey.

That afternoon, Trey, Isaac, and some of the guys from the B team were running drills against the rest of the starters and some other B team players.

Coach T blew his whistle to start the drill. Isaac and Trey and their teammates jogged up the court.

Isaac stopped at the top of the key and Trey cut around to the right. He faked out his defender at the three-point line and caught a perfect pass.

He spun, faked a drive, and shot. Three points!

"Nice shot, Trey," Coach T said. "And nice moves. You really left Dwayne in the dust with that fake."

Dwayne shook his head. "Aw, come on, Coach!" Dwayne said. "I'll get him next time."

The others laughed. Coach T glanced at his watch, and then at the clock over the doors. Then he blew his whistle again.

"That's it for today, gentlemen," he called out. "Hit the showers. Except you, Trey."

"Ooh," a few of the other players said. "Trey's in trouble!"

"You getting cut, Trey?" Isaac joked. He hit Trey on the back as he walked past.

"Right," Trey said. "I'm the captain, remember? He just wants to talk to me about how to make sure you don't blow the game for us this week."

Isaac laughed and headed into the locker room. The coach walked over to Trey, carrying his clipboard and flipping through some papers.

"So, this week we play Eastlake," Coach Turnbull said. "Any thoughts about the game?"

Trey scratched his head. "Last year we handled them easily," Trey said. "They probably have some good new players, but Joey Hotchsin is in high school now, and so is Paul Birk. Those two were their best players by far."

The coach nodded. "That's true," he said. "But I'm hearing an awful lot about this talented sixth grader named Pete Smith. Ever heard of him?"

"Yes," Trey said quietly. "He's my cousin. My dad's brother's son."

"I thought so," Coach T replied. "Are you two close?"

Trey shrugged. "We play a lot of two-on-two," he said. "Or we used to, anyway. This weekend we played one-on-one, against each other."

"Is Pete a good player?" the coach asked.

Trey shrugged again. "He's all right," he said. For some reason, he didn't feel like bragging about his cousin. He would have a week before, though. He used to be proud of how good his little cousin was with the ball.

"All right, thanks," the coach said. "And hey, will it be weird playing against him? He's a starter, so you'll be guarding him. And he'll be guarding you."

Trey waved the coach off as he walked toward the locker room. "No worries," Trey assured him. "It will be just like any other game."

Chapter 5
SHOWED UP

Just before the game started on Wednesday night, Trey peered out of the locker room door. He spotted his father and Pete's father as they walked into the gym.

The two men talked for a moment at the door. Then, as Trey watched, they went to sit on opposite sides of the court. Trey's dad went to the Wildcats side, while Pete's went to the visitors side.

Then the Eastlake team came jogging in to warm up on their end of the court.

Trey spotted his cousin in the front of the Eastlake team as they came in. He was waving and smiling at the crowd.

"What a show-off," Trey mumbled.

Dwayne Illy came up next to him. "Who?" he said. "The little guy?"

Trey nodded. "My cousin Pete," he said. "He thinks he's the best basketball player since Michael Jordan."

Dwayne laughed. "He's in sixth grade and he starts?" he asked. "He probably is pretty good, huh?"

The Eastlake team started shooting around. Dwayne and Trey watched Pete. He was doing plenty of fancy dribbling and showing off.

"Yeah, he's pretty good all right," Dwayne said.

Then the loudspeaker clicked on. The eighth-grade class president, Tina Hawk, took the microphone. "And now, the Westfield Wildcats!" she announced.

Coach T stood up and clapped as the other four starting Wildcats stood up. Trey groaned and slowly got to his feet.

"Cheer up, Trey," Dwayne said. "We got this game, easy."

Trey nodded and jogged with the other starters out to the court. They lined up for some quick layups. Trey made his shot easily. Then the Wildcats and the Eastlake team got ready to play.

The Wildcats got possession first, thanks to PJ Harris, their very tall starting center.

PJ tapped the ball to Isaac Roth. Right away, the Wildcats moved to the basket.

Isaac dribbled at the top of the key. The Eastlake player guarding him waited for him to start the play.

Trey watched Isaac as Pete stuck close to him. Pete was all smiles, but Trey was feeling the pressure of a new game. He didn't look Pete in the eye.

Isaac raised three fingers, and Trey faked toward the basket. Then he cut back toward Isaac. He thought he had lost Pete.

Isaac thought so too, so he passed to Trey. Just then, Pete ran past, knocking the ball away from Trey. Pete quickly dribbled toward the Eastlake basket. Trey tried to get back on defense in time, but Pete was already at the basket.

Pete made the layup easily for the first two points of the game. The score was two to nothing, Eastlake.

The crowd on the visitor side cheered and hollered. Someone yelled, "Way to go, Smith!"

It was only a few seconds into the game, and Trey's little cousin had already humiliated him.

Chapter 6
BLOWING IT

Trey threw in the ball to Isaac to start play after the first basket.

The coach and Trey's teammates were still in good spirits. Coach T walked along the sideline, clapping.

"Look alive out there, guys," Coach T shouted. "Let's make sure that's the last time Eastlake steals from us in this game, okay?"

Trey hustled to his spot down the court.

I can't believe I let Pete get that steal, he thought. *Well, I'll show him who the better player is.*

Isaac called a give-and-go, but Trey didn't want to just pass the ball back to Isaac. Trey wanted to be the one to score the next basket. He had to show Pete he was just as good.

When the pass came, Trey dodged Pete, caught the pass, and went straight to the hoop. With a little fancy dribbling through his legs, Trey went up for the layup.

But too many Eastlake players were on him, including Pete. There just wasn't room.

Trey tried to lay the ball up underhanded, but missed. The ball slammed into the bottom of the backboard.

The whole basket shook. Then the ball went flying out of bounds.

"Trey!" Isaac called out. "That was a give-and-go. Why'd you drive?"

Trey looked over at the bench. The coach looked angry, and Trey felt like an idiot. So far, Pete looked like a great player. Trey lost a pass and blew a layup.

Eastlake started their possession. Trey hoped their point guard would pass to Pete. That way, Trey would have a chance to make up for his mistakes and show up his cousin at the same time.

But Eastlake's point guard glanced toward Pete, then passed to their small forward. Eastlake's small forward drove hard to the basket, so Trey fell off Pete and doubled up on the forward.

"Trey!" Coach T called from the sideline. "Get back to your man!"

But it was too late. The Eastlake small forward cut his drive short. He passed the ball under his other arm — right to Pete Smith.

Pete was wide open. He casually raised the ball and sank a perfect shot from downtown. Three more points for Eastlake!

Chapter 7
TALKING TRASH

On Westfield's next possession, Isaac
held the ball at the top of the key a
little longer than usual. Trey was open.
Everyone could see that. He was the only
Wildcat who'd been able to shake his man
long enough to get open for a pass.

Trey bounced around, dodging Pete,
staying open, but Isaac still held the ball.
He looked at the other three Wildcats on
the court.

Isaac probably thinks I'll mess up again, Trey thought. But Trey didn't plan to try to show off this time. He'd play it just like he was supposed to.

I'm not going to make that mistake a third time, he thought.

Finally, Isaac passed to Trey. Trey caught the pass easily, then faked toward the hoop.

Pete darted alongside to keep up, but Trey stopped short. His sneakers squeaked on the wood floor as he drew up and shot. Two points!

"How's that?" Trey said when Pete turned to face him. "Now who's better?"

Pete smirked at his older cousin.

"Nothing to say now, huh?" Trey said.

Pete shook his head and jogged away to start the next possession.

"That's right," Trey called after him. "Walk away. Because you know you got nothing!"

"Trey!" the coach suddenly snapped from the sidelines. "On the bench, right now!" Coach Turnbull was red in the face and out of breath. Trey swallowed. He didn't like it when the coach was angry.

"Do I need to take you out of this game, Trey?" Coach T asked.

Trey sighed. "No," he said.

"You said it wouldn't be a problem playing against your cousin," Coach Turnbull went on. "But I see now that it is a problem. As a matter of fact, it's looking like a very big problem."

"No, honest, Coach," Trey said. "It's not a problem. I was just kidding around."

The coach just stared at him.

"For real, Coach T," Trey continued. "I just made all those mistakes before, and I was excited to score. That's all."

"Speaking of those mistakes, those weren't like you, Trey," Coach T said. "You're normally a reliable player. You stick to the plan and score points. It's why you're the captain of the team."

"I'm sorry, Coach," Trey said. "It won't happen again, honest."

The coach sighed. "All right," he said. "You get one more chance out there. No more trash talking, and no more crazy chances. Follow the plan and the Wildcats win, got it?"

"I got it," Trey said. The ref blew the whistle and Trey ran out to join the game.

On defense, Trey stayed calm, but he couldn't stop thinking about how mad Coach Turnbull had been. The coach never got mad at Trey. Sure, he sometimes hollered at Dwayne Illy for showing off, or at PJ for goofing around during practice. But Trey? He was the team captain.

This is all Pete's fault, Trey thought. *I'll get him back.*

Eastlake drove up the court. This time, their forward found their center, who had posted up. But his shot was off.

The rebound came right to Trey. He shoveled it to Isaac and the Westfield fans cheered as they headed back up the court.

Isaac raised a fist as he ran up. Trey followed the play and hustled to his spot just as Pete came up on him.

Now's my chance, Trey thought.

Trey caught the pass, then spun and knocked into Pete. He only hit him with his shoulder, but the ref spotted it. A whistle went off just as Trey laid up the ball for a basket.

"No points," the ref called out. "Charging on Westfield Smith. Eastlake Smith will take two shots."

"What?!" Trey shouted at the ref, but Coach T had a hand on his shoulder right away.

"Bench," Coach T said. "Now."

Chapter 8
CHAMPIONSHIP PLAYERS

Trey sat out the rest of the first half. The second string guard couldn't keep up with Pete at all. After a few minutes, Eastlake's lead had grown to fifteen points.

Trey knew that his dad and his uncle were looking at him. But he didn't look back at them. He hung his head and stared at the gym floor.

During halftime, the other Wildcats just glared at him.

I know what they're all thinking, Trey thought. *How is this joker the team captain?*

At the moment, Trey wasn't so sure himself. He knew he had screwed up, but he wasn't sure how to fix it.

The coach went over a few plays and corrected a few mistakes. Then he sent the team out to run a few drills. Trey started to follow everyone else.

"Um, hold on a minute, Trey," the coach said. He put a hand on his shoulder.

"Yeah?" Trey said. He turned to face the coach.

Coach T pointed at the locker room bench. "Have a seat," he said.

Trey dropped onto the bench. "Don't you want me to get out there to do drills with the other guys?" Trey asked.

"Trey, I'm not going to start you in the second half," Coach T said.

Trey nodded sadly. "I'm not surprised," he said.

"Until you cool off," the coach went on, "I'm not going to put you back in. Is that clear?"

Trey sighed loudly. "Yeah," he said. "It's clear."

"All right," the coach said. "Then get out there and hit the wood until you're acting like yourself."

Trey grunted and got to his feet. Then he jogged out of the locker room and went straight to the bench. He sat down next to Daniel Friedland, the second string small forward.

"Hey," Daniel said.

Trey didn't even look at Daniel. He just grunted. He couldn't stop watching Pete, who was on the court, shooting layups with his team.

Just before the second half started, Pete looked over at the Wildcats bench. He and Trey made eye contact, and Pete smiled.

Trey nearly screamed. He couldn't believe Pete was smiling. Trey wasn't starting. This was all Pete's fault, and Pete had the nerve to laugh about it!

"Hi, son," a voice suddenly said. Trey turned around. His father and Pete's father were standing behind him.

"Oh hi, Dad," Trey said. "Hi, Uncle Theo. Enjoying the game?"

"No, we're not, Trey," Dad replied.

Trey looked at his feet.

"You know, Trey," Uncle Theo said, "when your father and I were in college, basketball wasn't our game."

"So?" Trey said.

"We played baseball," Uncle Theo went on. "And since we're close in age and went to different colleges, we played each other a few times."

Dad's face suddenly lit up. "Remember that one game, Theo?" he said.

Uncle Theo nodded. "Sure," he said. "The championship, senior year. Biggest game I ever played in."

"Trey, I wish you could have seen it," Dad said. "It was the old classic scenario. The bottom of the ninth inning . . ."

"Two outs," Uncle Theo put in. "And I was pitching to the best hitter at State."

"Me!" Dad said. "We were down by two runs. There were two men on base, and I was up. The pressure was on."

"And hey," Uncle Theo said. "I was a good pitcher, don't forget."

"Best in the league," Trey's dad admitted.

"A hush fell over the stands," Uncle Theo said. "The whole stadium was on the edge of their seats."

"What pitch did you throw?" Trey's dad asked. "Was it a slider?"

"Nope. Breaking fastball," Uncle Theo said. "I had a great breaking pitch."

Neither man said anything for a few moments. Trey heard the ref blow his whistle to get the basketball players ready for the second half.

"So?" Trey said finally. "Who won the championship?"

The two men looked at each other. Then they burst out laughing.

"That's the thing, Trey," his father said.

"We can never remember!" Uncle Theo finished.

The two men laughed again. Then Trey's father looked at him.

"Get the idea, son?" Dad asked seriously.

Trey nodded. "Yeah," he said. "I get the idea."

Chapter 9
WHO WON?

The second half began. Trey tapped the coach on the shoulder.

"Hey, Coach T," Trey said. "I'm sorry for acting like such a jerk in the first half. I'm cooled off now. I'd like to play."

The coach looked at Trey for a long moment. "All right," he said. "Next stop in play, you're going in. Don't make me regret this decision."

After a few moments, the whistle blew. The coach patted Trey on the back, so he jogged onto the court to replace the second-string shooting guard.

"Hey, cuz," Pete said when Trey came up to him.

"Hey, Pete," Trey replied. He put out his hand. "No hard feelings?"

Pete shook his cousin's hand. "Of course not," he said. "We going to play some basketball now?"

"Definitely," Trey said. Both cousins smiled as play began again.

Isaac Roth got the ball to Trey right away. Trey faked a drive, then drew up and shot from behind the three-point line.

"Yes," he said as the shot fell. He heard the crowd cheering for him.

"Nice shot," Pete said.

Eastlake's point guard got the ball to Pete. After a pump that left Trey faked out, Pete drove to the hoop.

Trey recovered quickly and caught up to his cousin. With a burst of speed, he was able to knock the ball away from Pete and out of bounds.

"Eastlake ball," the ref called out. He handed the ball to Eastlake's point guard to throw in.

The point guard found Pete again right away. This time, Pete faked the drive and took a quick shot for two points. Trey was totally fooled.

"Wow," Trey said. "You really got me that time, little cousin."

"Plenty of time left in the half," Pete said.

Trey smiled as the two of them headed back up court. "You know it," he said.

Chapter 10
TWO ON TWO

At the park the next weekend, Pete and Trey were playing two-on-two against a couple of guys from Josette. They'd already won three games that morning, and it wasn't even lunchtime yet.

"Right here, cuz," Trey called to Pete.

"Get open!" Pete called back.

The player from Josette was taller than Pete, and he had him stopped.

Trey spun to his left, then darted across the key. His defender tripped up and Pete found Trey with a fast pass. Trey laid it up for the game-winning point.

"All right!" Pete said. The cousins high-fived at the foul line.

"Any more takers?" Pete said to some other kids watching. No one replied.

"That's fine," Uncle Theo said, walking over. "It's time for lunch anyway."

"We've got burgers and chicken," Dad added, "hot off the grill."

Trey picked up the basketball. Then he and Pete jogged over to the picnic table. One of the boys from Josette called over to them as they were about to eat.

"Hey, you two!" the kid said. "Don't you two go to Westfield and Eastlake?"

"Yeah," Trey replied. "So?"

"Well, didn't your teams play each other this week?" the Josette boy asked.

"Yes," Pete called back.

"So who won?" the boy said.

Trey and Pete looked at their dads, then at each other. They turned to the boy from Josette and replied together with a shrug, "We don't remember!"

THE AUTHOR
ERIC STEVENS

15

ERIC STEVENS LIVES IN ST. PAUL, MINNESOTA WITH HIS WIFE, DOG, AND SON. HE IS STUDYING TO BECOME A TEACHER. SOME OF HIS FAVORITE THINGS INCLUDE PIZZA AND VIDEO GAMES. SOME OF HIS LEAST FAVORITE THINGS INCLUDE OLIVES AND SHOVELING SNOW.

WHEN SEAN TIFFANY WAS GROWING UP, HE LIVED ON A SMALL ISLAND OFF THE COAST OF MAINE. EVERY DAY UNTIL HE GRADUATED FROM HIGH SCHOOL, HE HAD TO TAKE A BOAT TO GET TO SCHOOL! SEAN HAS A PET CACTUS NAMED JIM.

24

THE ILLUSTRATOR
SEAN TIFFANY

GLOSSARY

advantage (ad-VAN-tij)—something that helps or is useful

challenger (CHAL-uhnj-ur)—someone who is trying to beat you

defender (di-FEN-dur)—a player whose job is to protect the basket

humiliated (hyoo-MIL-ee-ate-id)—embarrassed

possession (puh-ZESH-uhn)—control of the ball

preview (PREE-vyoo)—a hint or viewing before something happens

reliable (ri-LYE-uh-buhl)—dependable

scenario (suh-NAIR-ee-oh)—an outline of events that might happen in a situation

talented (TAL-uhnt-id)—having skill or ability

DISCUSSION QUESTIONS

1. What are some things that Trey could have done besides get upset when he played against Pete?

2. Do you think cousins should be allowed to play against each other? Why or why not?

3. What did Trey and Pete learn from their dads?

WRITING PROMPTS

1. Write about your favorite relative. Why do you like that person?

2. Each year, the Smith family gets together. What traditions does your family have? Write about them.

3. Have you ever had to play against a friend or relative? What happened? How did you feel about it?

MORE ABOUT SHOOTING GUARDS

In this book, Trey Smith is the shooting guard for the Westfield Wildcats. Check out these quick facts about shooting guards.

* Shooting guards are usually shorter and quicker than centers or forwards.

* In the NBA, the average shooting guard is between 6 foot 4 inches and 6 foot 8 inches tall.

* A shooting guard's main job is to score points for his or her team. Shooting guards also need to be good at passing, and it can be very helpful for them to be good at ball-handling.

* Famous shooting guards have included Kobe Bryant, Reggie Miller, Allen Iverson, Michael Jordan, Tracy McGrady, Clyde Drexler, and Brandon Roy.